A Note to Parents and Caregivers:

With a focus on math, science, and social studies, *Read-it!* Readers support both the learning of content information and the extension of more complex reading skills. They encourage the development of problem-solving skills that help children expand their thinking.

 The PURPLE LEVEL presents basic topics and objects using high frequency words and simple language patterns.

 The RED LEVEL presents familiar topics using common words and repeating sentence patterns.

 The BLUE LEVEL presents new ideas using a larger vocabulary and varied sentence structure.

 The YELLOW LEVEL presents more challenging ideas, a broad vocabulary, and wide variety in sentence structure.

 The GREEN LEVEL presents more complex ideas, an extended vocabulary range, and expanded language structures.

 The ORANGE LEVEL presents a wide range of ideas and concepts using challenging vocabulary and complex language structures.

When sharing a content focused book with your child, read to find out facts and concepts, pausing often to restate and talk about the new information. The realistic story format provides an opportunity to talk about the language used, and to learn about reading to problem-solve for information. Encourage children to measure, make maps, and consider other situations that allow them to apply what they are learning.

There is no right or wrong way to share books with children. Find time to read and share new learning with your child, and pass on the legacy of literacy.

Adria F. Klein, Ph.D.
Professor Emeritus
California State University
San Bernardino, California

Editor: Jill Kalz
Designers: Abbey Fitzgerald and Tracy Davies
Page Production: Melissa Kes
Art Director: Nathan Gassman
Associate Managing Editor: Christianne Jones
The illustrations in this book were created digitally.

Picture Window Books
5115 Excelsior Boulevard
Suite 232
Minneapolis, MN 55416
877-845-8392
www.picturewindowbooks.com

Printed in the United States of America.

Library of Congress Cataloging-in-Publication Data
Blackaby, Susan.
Lost on Owl Lane / by Susan Blackaby ; illustrated by Amy Bailey Muehlenhardt.
p. cm. — (Read-it! readers. Social Studies)
Summary: Jessie is new to her neighborhood, and when she needs to find her way to
the library, she asks for help from her neighbor, Sara, who uses a computer to make
a map then teaches Jessie how to use it. Includes activities.
ISBN-13: 978-1-4048-2333-4 (library binding)
ISBN-10: 1-4048-2333-6 (library binding)
[1. Map reading—Fiction. 2. Neighborhood—Fiction. 3. Dogs—Fiction.]
I. Muehlenhardt, Amy Bailey, 1974– ill. II. Title.
PZ7.B5318Los 2007
[E]—dc22   2007005357

Lost on
OWL LANE

by Susan Blackaby
illustrated by Amy Bailey Muehlenhardt

Special thanks to our advisers for their expertise:

Mark Harrower, Ph.D.
Assistant Professor, Department of Geography
University of Wisconsin, Madison

Adria F. Klein, Ph.D.
Professor Emeritus, California State University
San Bernardino, California

PiCTURE WiNDOW BOOKS
Minneapolis, Minnesota

When Jessie first moved to Owl Lane, she felt lost all of the time. But she was lucky. She lived next door to an older kid named Sara.

Sara was cool. She had a laptop computer. She had a cute dog named Pixie. Best of all, she knew her way around the neighborhood. Whenever Jessie had a question about how to get somewhere, Sara had an answer.

"Hi, Sara," said Jessie, walking onto Sara's porch. "My mom forgot her date book this morning. She's working at the library right now. I need to take it to her. Can you tell me how to get there?"

"You bet," said Sara. "I can even give you a map."

Sara logged on to her computer. She found a map of the neighborhood and printed it out.

"This is Owl Lane," said Sara, pointing to a gray dotted line. She put a red X on the map. "And this is where you live."

"Why doesn't Owl Lane look like the other streets?" Jessie asked.

"It's a gravel road," Sara answered. "On this map, gray dotted lines are gravel roads. Solid cream-colored lines are paved streets. See this box in the corner? It's called a key. The key shows what all of the lines and shapes mean."

Key

▭	paved city road
– – – – –	gravel road
═══	bridge
~~	creek
┼┼┼┼	railroad track
‹‹‹‹‹	one-way street

Jessie looked at the key and all of its symbols. Then she pointed to some long and short lines on the map. They looked like a fence. "The railroad tracks!" she said.

"Correct!" Sara said. "You are going to walk in the opposite direction of the railroad tracks. At the end of Owl Lane, turn left. That street is called Creek Drive. Go two blocks on Creek Drive to First Street."

"Is that the corner with the big pine tree?" asked Jessie.

"Yes," said Sara. She drew a tree symbol on the map. "The pine tree is a good landmark. A landmark is something that stands out. When you see it, you know you are in the right spot."

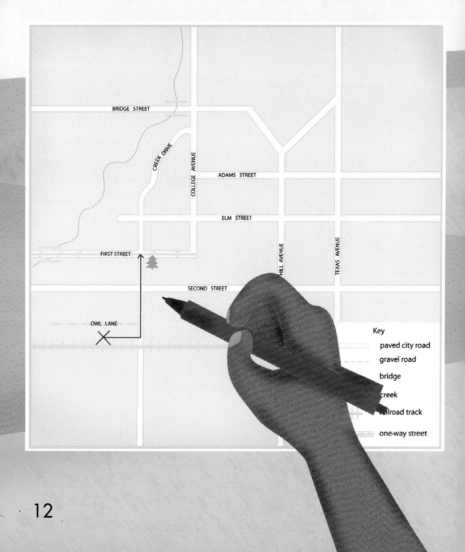

"Could my brother's bike be a landmark?" Jessie asked. "It's orange. It really stands out!"

"No, the best landmarks are things that don't move," Sara explained. "Trees, buildings, and big rocks make good landmarks."

"What should I do when I get to the big pine tree?" Jessie asked.

"Turn right," Sara said. "You'll be on First Street. Follow First Street until it ends, and then turn left. That's College Avenue. The library is right down the street." Sara smiled and put a library symbol on the map. "Got it?"

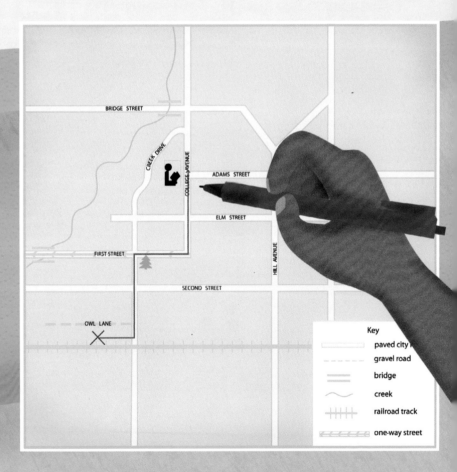

"I think so," Jessie said as she slowly folded the map.

Pixie started to whine and wag her tail. Sara got an idea.

"I'll go with you, Jessie," Sara said. "We can take Pixie for a walk."

Jessie, Sara, and Pixie walked to the end of Owl Lane. Jessie read the map and led the way. They turned left on Creek Drive. They turned right at the pine tree. They turned left at the end of First Street.

When they came to the intersection at College Avenue and Elm Street, Jessie stopped. "My school is near here," she said, pointing down the street. "But the bus goes a different way to get there. It doesn't turn by the big pine tree like we did."

"First Street is a one-way street," said Sara. "Cars and other vehicles aren't allowed to turn right by the big pine tree. But walkers can go any way they want."

Jessie looked at the map. First Street was a cream-colored line with arrows in it. The key said it was a one-way street. Sara was right!

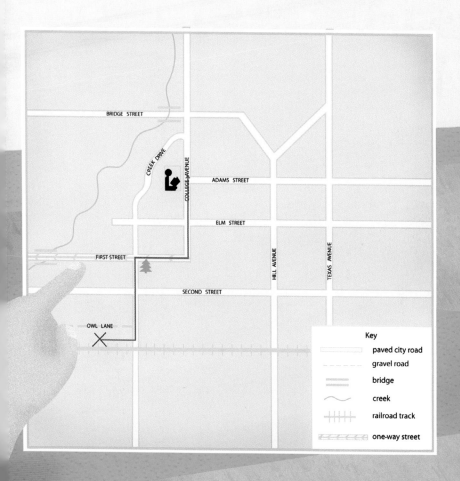

At the library, Jessie went to the main desk and dropped off her mom's date book. Sara and Pixie waited outside.

"Job completed," said Jessie, walking back out. "Now where should we go?"

Pixie started to whine and wag her tail.
"Let's take Pixie to the park," said Sara.
"It's at the top of Hill Avenue." She put a park symbol on the map. "From here, we'll go right on Adams Street and then left on Hill Avenue. At the fork, we'll go to the right."

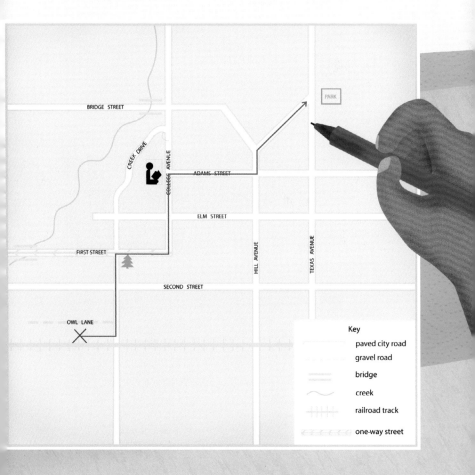

So, Jessie, Sara, and Pixie walked along Adams Street. It was a beautiful, sunny day. They couldn't wait to get to the park. But as soon as they turned up Hill Avenue, Jessie got quiet. She walked with her head down.

"Jessie, are you OK?" Sara asked.

"I'm looking for it," Jessie said.

"Looking for what?" Sara asked.

"The fork. I'm looking for the fork," said Jessie with a worried look.

Sara laughed. She told Jessie to look at the map. "See how the road splits and makes a letter Y?" she said. "That is called a fork."

Jessie laughed, too. "Oh," she said. "I suppose a real fork would be a funny landmark, wouldn't it?"

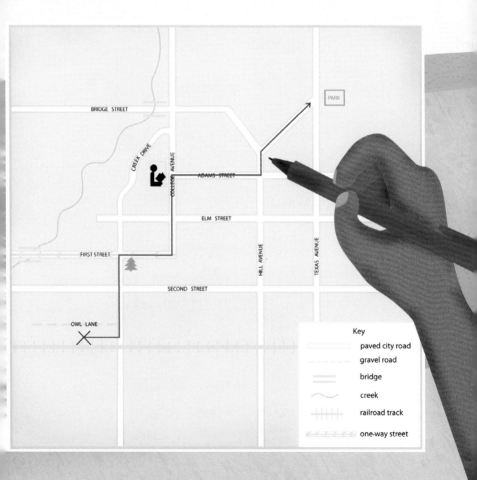

Jessie, Sara, and Pixie had a great time at the park. Pixie played with all kinds of dogs. In no time at all, she was a dirty mess.

"Pixie, you need a bath," said Sara. "We can stop at Shampooch on the way home. It's on the corner of Texas Avenue and Elm Street."

Jessie looked at the symbol Sara had drawn on the map. "Easy!" she said. "To get there, we go straight down Texas Avenue."

"Lead the way!" said Sara.

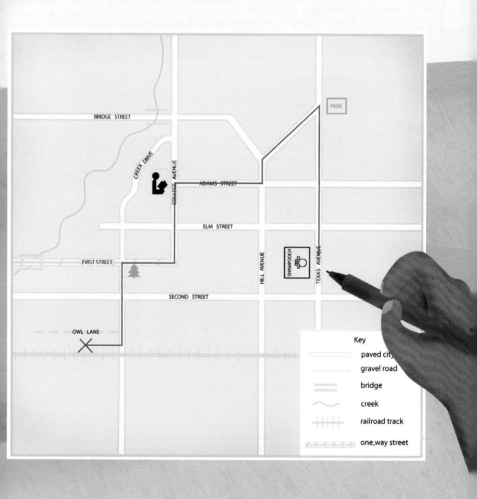

BRIDGE STREET

CREEK DRIVE

COLLEGE AVENUE

ADAMS STREET

ELM STREET

HILL AVENUE

SHAMPOOCH

TEXAS AVENUE

PARK

FIRST STREET

SECOND STREET

OWL LANE

Key
— paved city
- - - gravel road
= bridge
∼ creek
+++ railroad track
one-way street

At Shampooch, Pixie got washed from her nose to her tail. She got rinsed and fluffed. She got a big red bow, too.

As the group headed for home, Jessie looked at the map again. Sara had drawn another symbol on it while Jessie wasn't looking.

"If we follow Texas Avenue to Second Street and turn right, we'll go past Two Scoops," Jessie said. "We can get ice-cream cones."

"Hey!" said Sara. "You really know your way around this neighborhood."

Jessie smiled and said, "It's easy if you have a map and a little bit of help."

Activity: Looking at Your Neighborhood

What you need:

- a map of your town or neighborhood (to find one, check the Web or ask an adult; some phone books have maps inside them, too)

What you do:

1. Find your house on the map. You may need to ask an adult for help.

2. Now, look around your house on the map. What are the names of the streets in your neighborhood? Can you find your school? Can you find a park? Do you see any railroad tracks or one-way streets? What symbols does the map key include?

Glossary

direction—the point toward which something can face
key—the part of a map that explains what the map's symbols (for example,
    lines, shapes, and pictures) mean
landmark—something that stands out, such as a big tree or a building
symbols—things that stand for something else

To Learn More

At the Library

Bullard, Lisa. *My Neighborhood: Places and Faces.* Minneapolis: Picture
    Window Books, 2003.
Caseley, Judith. *On the Town: A Community Adventure.* New York:
    Greenwillow Books, 2002.
Leedy, Loreen. *Mapping Penny's World.* New York: Henry Holt, 2000.

On the Web

FactHound offers a safe, fun way to find Web sites related to this book.
All of the sites on FactHound have been researched by our staff.

1. Visit *www.facthound.com*
2. Type in this special code: 1404823336
3. Click on the FETCH IT button.

Your trusty FactHound will fetch the best sites for you!

Look for all of the books in the *Read-it!* Readers: Social Studies series:

The Carnival Committee (geography: map skills)
Groceries for Grandpa (geography: map skills)
Lost on Owl Lane (geography: map skills)
Todd's Fire Drill (geography: map skills)